To ....

HAPPY HALLOWEEN!

Love, ...

....

TRICK OR TREAT IN TEXAS

Written by Eric James
Illustrated by Karl West

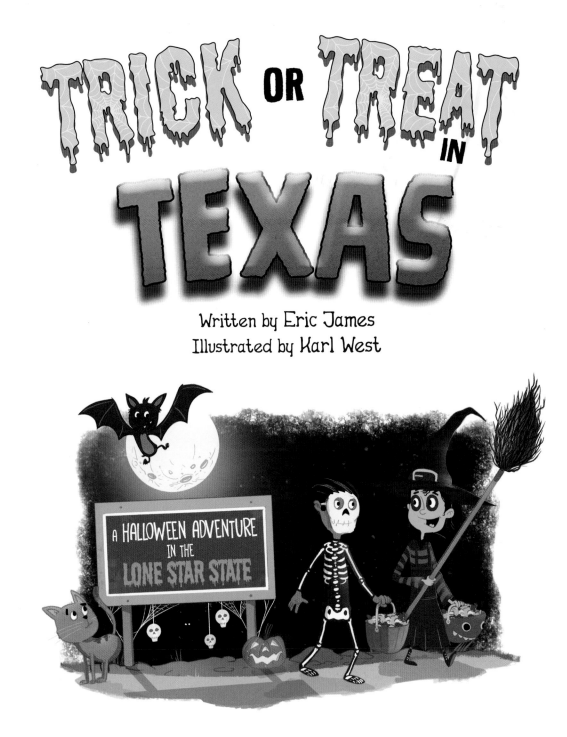

A HALLOWEEN ADVENTURE
IN THE
LONE STAR STATE

sourcebooks
jabberwocky

The full moon's out on Halloween.
The sky is starry bright.
Above the state of Texas
appears an eerie light.

LONE STAR STATE
SPOOKY BALL

CANDY BAR

TOYS

HILL COUNTRY
BOOKSTORE

CORPUS CHRISTI   LANDA PARK

It darts behind the scattered clouds.
It zips from town to town.
It hovers over San Antonio,
then slowly heads on d
o
w
n.

SAN ANTONIO RIVER WALK

A ramp shoots out. A hatch appears.
Smoke pours into the air.
A chilling alien silhouette
gives owls and wolves a scare!

IT STEPS OUT OF THE THICK WHITE FOG.
ITS SKIN IS NEON GREEN.
THIS ALIEN IS, WITHOUT A DOUBT...

LANDA PARK